12/17
361

Cold Whispers II

TRAPPED in the ABANDONED HOSPITAL

by Dee Phillips

illustrated by Anthony Resto

BEARPORT
PUBLISHING

New York, New York

Credits
Cover, © OFFFSTOCK/Shutterstock.

Publisher: Kenn Goin
Editor: Jessica Rudolph
Creative Director: Spencer Brinker

Library of Congress Cataloging-in-Publication Data in process at time of publication (201
Library of Congress Control Number: 2016020326
ISBN-13: 978-1-944102-31-9

For more information, write to Bearport Publishing Company, Inc.,
45 West 21st Street, Suite 3B, New York, New York 10010.
Printed in the United States of America.

10 9 8 7 6 5 4 3 2 1

Contents

CHAPTER 1

Hospital Hill

Grace closed her math book. *Phew.* Her homework was finally finished. Now it was time for her favorite part of the evening. She looked at her dog, Bobby, who was dozing on the bed.

"It's time for your walk," said Grace. Bobby opened his eyes, and his tail began to thump with excitement.

"Let's go!" she said. Bobby jumped up and bounded down the stairs toward the front door.

Since Grace had turned thirteen, she'd been allowed to walk Bobby on her own every day.

"Grace, honey," shouted Dad from the kitchen. "It's starting to get dark. Please don't stay out too long."

Grace put on her jacket and clipped Bobby's leash to his red collar. The little dog's brown eyes sparkled with joy. Bobby was Grace's best friend in the whole world. Her dad had brought him home from an **animal shelter** when she was just four years old. Since then, they'd been almost **inseparable**.

Out on the street, Grace shivered. It was a cool evening and the sun was already going down.

"Do you want to go up the hill?" she asked the little dog. Bobby wagged his tail. Grace knew that meant yes.

At the end of the street, they turned onto a long, steep road called Hospital Hill. It was named for the old **sanatorium** that stood at the top of the hill.

Up and up they climbed. Near the top of the hill, the hospital loomed into view. It had been closed for more than fifty years and was surrounded by a chain-link fence.

Grace stopped walking to catch her breath. She looked at the **dilapidated** old building. Its dark windows seemed to look back at her, like empty black eyes.

The kids at school loved to tell stories about the sanatorium. The most terrifying tale was about a boy who dared to enter the building one night and was never seen again! Grace didn't really believe the story. But it gave her the shivers to think about it.

A sudden gust of cold wind rattled a rusty "KEEP OUT: DANGER" sign that clung to the fence. Grace was just about to turn back toward home when . . .

Grrrrr. Woof! Woof! Grrrrr. Bobby became tense. He was growling and barking at something in a patch of weeds.

"Bobby, shush!" shouted Grace.

Suddenly, a black cat shot out from its hiding place in the weeds. Bobby pulled hard on his leash, and Grace lost her grip. The leash slipped out of her hands, and Bobby took off!

"Bobby, no! Come back!" cried Grace.

The black cat squeezed under the fence. Then it raced across the pavement in front of the hospital. Bobby, who was right behind the cat, quickly wriggled under the fence, too.

"Bobby. Come back! Come back!" screamed Grace.

The cat flew up the steps to the hospital's main doorway. A large section of the old wooden doors had rotted away. The cat leaped through a hole in the rotting wood and disappeared inside. Seconds later, Bobby followed.

"Bobby. Oh no." Grace's voice was just a whisper. "Please come back."

Grace could hear Bobby's excited barking coming from inside the hospital. Her stomach flipped over with panic. She swallowed hard and told herself that she would NOT cry.

"Bobby! Bobby! Time for dinner!" she cried hopefully. But after a minute passed, Grace was sure he wasn't going to come back. To her **dismay**, she noticed how quickly the sunlight had faded. She looked at the KEEP OUT: DANGER sign. Then she thought of her little dog in the vast, empty building.

Grace went up to the fence. She tugged and tugged at the spot where the animals had squeezed through. Finally, there was just enough space for her to crawl under the fence.

As she stood up, brushing dirt from her jeans, she looked up at the rows of windows. The panic in her stomach turned to fear. She felt as if the hospital was daring her to step inside.

"It's just an old building," she said out loud. "An old, empty building." Then she took a deep breath and walked quickly toward the spooky abandoned hospital.

CHAPTER 2
A Night in the Sanatorium

Grace walked up the crumbling stone steps to the hospital's main entrance. A rusted chain and padlock held the doors together, but Grace was able to squeeze through a crack between the heavy doors.

The hospital's main hallway was lit by an eerie whitish-blue light. Grace realized it was moonlight shining through the windows. Dead leaves and **shards** of broken glass littered the dusty floor. The walls of the hospital were cracked and the paint was coming off in layers. It made Grace think of dead, peeling skin.

"Bobby?" Grace said hopefully. Her voice sounded tiny and afraid. "Bobby. Where are you?" She listened, but could hear only silence.

To Grace's left and right were long corridors. They seemed to go on forever, disappearing into darkness. She began to creep along one of the corridors. On one side of the hallway were tall windows filled with jagged glass. On the other side were many doors.

Grace's footsteps were the only sound until, suddenly, she heard *squeak, rattle, squeak, rattle.* Slowly, a **gurney** rolled toward her out of the darkness—all on its own! Its tiny wheels made high-pitched squeaks with every turn. Grace stepped aside just before the gurney could bump into her. Then it stopped. Grace's heart was beating fast. She couldn't believe what she'd just seen. Had someone pushed the gurney toward her?

"Hello?" she said softly into the darkness. "Who's there?"

An icy breeze rattled the windowpanes. Dry leaves blew across the floor. Could the wind have blown the gurney along the corridor?

Grace's legs were shaking with fear, but she walked on.

What was that? Grace stopped. She was sure she'd heard a noise behind one of the doors to her left.

"Bobby?" she called out. Her voice echoed off the walls and the high ceiling.

The door was slightly **ajar**. Grace pushed it hard and it opened with a loud creak. She stepped into the room and saw walls lined with bookcases. A large desk stacked with books filled the center of the room. Grace figured the room must have once been a doctor's **study**.

She walked to the desk and looked at the books. The cover of each one was printed with the words *Hilltop Sanatorium* and a year. The oldest book had "1920" printed on the cover. The most recent said "1961." Carefully, she brushed a thick layer of dust from one of the books, titled:

HILLTOP SANATORIUM 1929

Grace opened the book. Its pages were filled with the names of hospital patients. The ink was faded, but beside each name she could just read the patient's age and **diagnosis**— and the day the patient died.

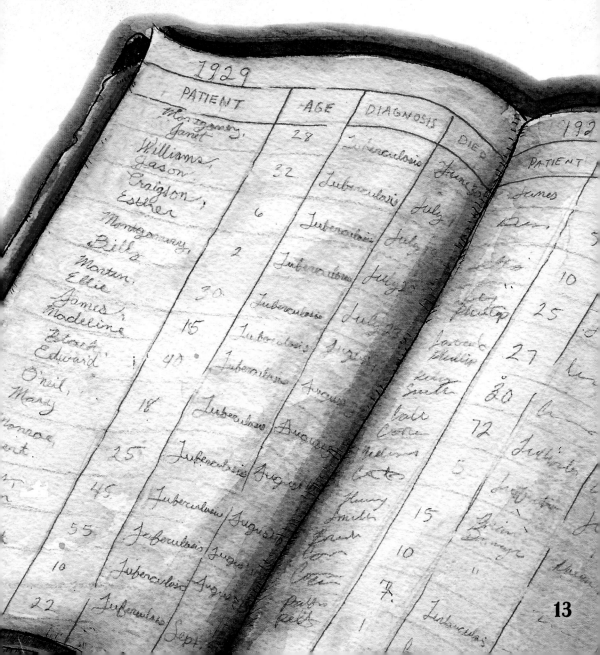

Grace felt the hairs on the back of her neck start to prickle. She had the strangest feeling she was being watched. Slowly, Grace turned to look behind her. For just a brief moment, she saw a shadowy shape in the doorway of the study. Then it was gone.

"Is someone there?" croaked Grace.

She slipped out of the study and looked up and down the corridor. Nothing. Grace knew that no matter how scared she felt, she had to keep searching for her dog.

She was edging slowly along the corridor when she heard a person coughing and wheezing behind a set of swinging doors. Then the coughing stopped, and the person began to cry.

Grace peered into the door's window and saw a long hospital **ward**. She pushed on one of the doors and it swung open.

"Hello?" she asked. "Does somebody need help?"

As soon as she stepped into the ward, the crying stopped.

A long row of narrow metal beds lined each wall. Grace slowly walked between them. Some beds were just rusting frames. Others were covered with thin mattresses. Then she noticed a movement on one of the beds in the middle of the ward.

Grace crept toward the bed. The mattress was bulging and moving. It seemed to be alive.

"Aaaarrrrrgggggg!" A loud scream erupted from Grace's mouth. Swarming in and out of the **decaying** mattress were rats—dozens and dozens of them!

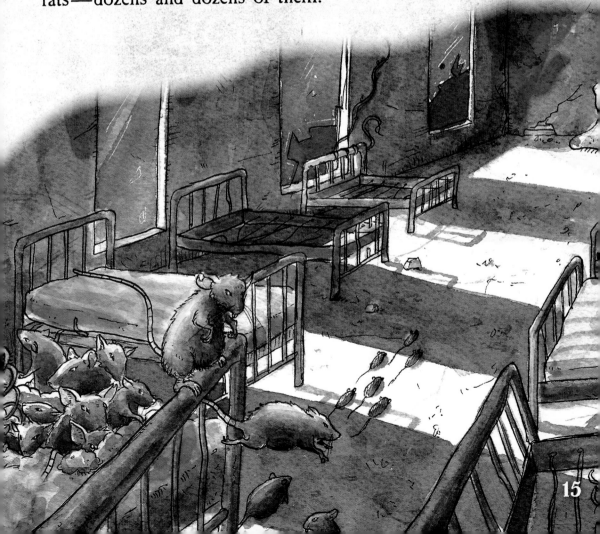

Grace backed away in horror. Then she felt something under her feet. She stepped aside and saw that it was a handkerchief. She noticed a dark, wet stain on the white cloth. Grace realized it was fresh blood!

Suddenly the terrible sound of wheezing and coughing seemed to be all around her. Grace ran back past the empty beds, out of the swinging doors, and into the corridor. She had to find Bobby and get out of this place—now!

"Bobby! Bobby!" she screamed as she ran.

At the very end of the hallway, she came to a pair of large, black doors. The doors were hanging loose on their hinges. Grace carefully squeezed between them and found herself in complete darkness.

Then she heard a soft whimper.

"Bobby?" she called. To her delight, she was answered by a small, weak *woof*!

Grace reached into her pocket, took out her cell phone, and turned on the phone's tiny flashlight. She was in a long, narrow tunnel that sloped away from her—as if it was leading underground. *Why would there be an underground tunnel in a hospital?* Grace wondered.

Up ahead, Grace could see the outline of a small dog. It was Bobby!

"Come here, boy!" she cried. But his leash was caught on a piece of metal that jutted out from the tunnel wall.

Grace carefully made her way along the tunnel. When she reached Bobby, she unhooked the leash from his collar to free him. As she hugged him, the little dog anxiously licked her face.

"You silly dog," Grace said, holding him tight. "How did you get yourself trapped in here?"

Carrying Bobby in her arms, Grace began to walk back along the tunnel. That's when she heard faint voices. The whispering was all around her.

"Get out. Get out."

"Don't let them take you down the tunnel."

Terrified, Grace began to run along the crumbling stone floor. Her foot got caught between the chunks of broken stone and she crashed to the ground, dropping Bobby. As her cell phone flew from her hand, it smashed on the stone floor and the flashlight went out.

Grace tried to free her foot, but the pain was unbearable. She scrambled in the dark for her cell phone, but it had slid out of reach.

"Help! Help!" she screamed into the darkness. But she knew there was no one around to help her.

"What am I going to do, Bobby?" Grace began to cry. The little dog gently licked her face. Then he turned his head and began to growl.

Grrrrrrrrr. Grrrrrrrrrrr. The fur on his back stood on end.

"What is it, Bobby?" Grace cried in panic.

In the darkness, Grace could just make out something moving toward them along the tunnel.

"Hello?" said Grace, her voice shaking. "Who's there?"

The shadowy shape moved closer and closer.

Grace pulled Bobby to her. A terrifying thought drifted into her mind.

There was once a boy who dared to go into the old hospital at night. He was never seen again . . . .

CHAPTER 3

The Death Tunnel

Shaking with fear, Grace huddled in the dark tunnel and hugged Bobby tightly. The shadowy shape grew closer. Grace realized it was a man wearing a white coat.

"Don't be afraid," said the man kindly. "I want to help you."

He knelt beside Grace. He was carrying a bag and a small lamp, the kind that Grace's dad used when he went fishing at night. He lit the lamp, and the dark tunnel flooded with warm, comforting light.

Grace could see that the man had neatly combed hair and a small black moustache.

"My name is Dr. Walter Akerson," he said. "What's your name?"

"It's Grace. Grace Scott," she answered shyly.

Bobby pressed his body to Grace and made a low growling noise.

"I didn't think anyone still worked here," said Grace. "I thought this place was abandoned."

The doctor looked sad.

"The hospital is no longer the place it once was," he said thoughtfully. "But some of us are still here to care for those who need help."

The doctor held up his lamp so he could see Grace's foot.

"How did you come to be in the death tunnel?" he asked.

A terrible shiver ran through Grace's body. *The death tunnel? What did he mean?*

The doctor looked into Grace's frightened face.

"Oh!" he said. "I must apologize, Grace. I didn't mean to alarm you. I don't like to hear the tunnel called that, but sadly, it does describe its purpose."

As he talked, Dr. Akerson carefully freed Grace's foot from the crumbling floor and took her shoe off. She **winced** in pain.

The doctor gently examined her ankle. Then he took a bandage and two small foot-shaped pieces of metal from his bag.

"I'm sorry, but your ankle is badly sprained, Grace," he said. "These metal **splints** will help support it."

Grace could feel the pain lessen as he strapped the splints to her ankle with the bandage. Then she remembered the book she'd seen in the doctor's study—the book filled with names.

"What happened to the patients here?" asked Grace.

"Most of the patients who came to Hilltop Sanatorium suffered from **tuberculosis**," said Dr. Akerson. "It's a terrible disease of the lungs. Patients had severe chest pain. They

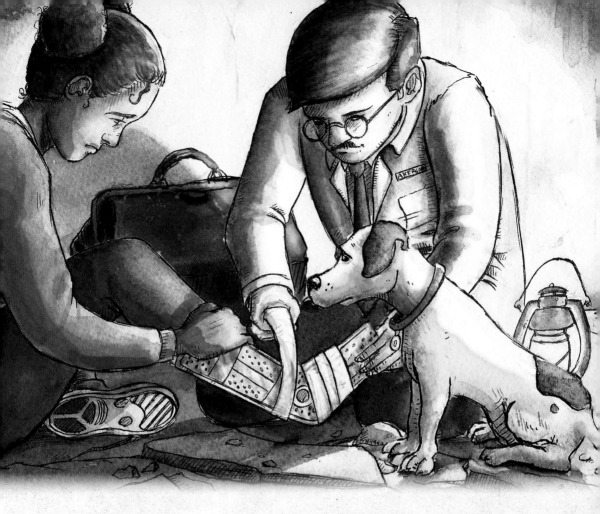

coughed up blood night and day and wasted away."

Grace noticed that the doctor looked sad again. "Thousands of people passed away here," he said. "They died slow, painful deaths."

Dr. Akerson looked into Grace's eyes. "We tried to help, but there was little that could be done to save them."

Grace thought back to the coughing and wheezing sounds she'd heard in the hospital ward—and the crying.

"After a person died, the doctors and nurses wanted to protect their patients from the awful truth," said Dr. Akerson. "They did not want the living to see the dead being carried from the hospital."

"The dead bodies were taken down this tunnel?" asked Grace.

"Yes," said Dr. Akerson. "The **undertakers** waited at the other end to collect them. The end of the tunnel is down the hill, far from the hospital." His voice faded away.

Grace looked down the tunnel.

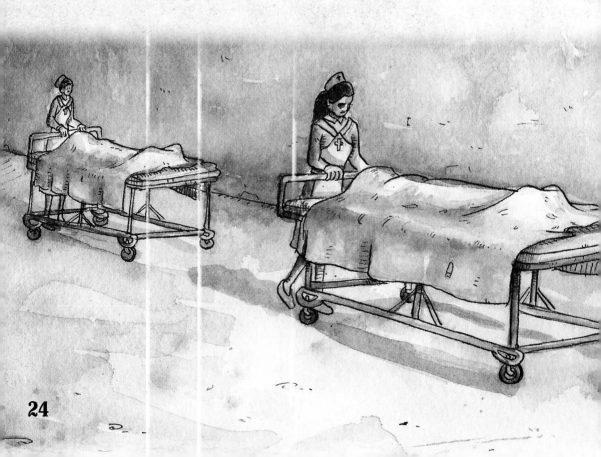

"The death tunnel," she whispered. She could hardly bear the thought of a final journey down the long, dark tunnel. She remembered the whispered voices: *"Don't let them take you down the tunnel."*

Dr. Akerson finished wrapping Grace's ankle.

"How does it feel?" he asked, smiling. "Have I been of help?"

Before Grace could answer, the light in the little lamp dimmed and went out. The tunnel was plunged into darkness.

Then Grace heard a familiar voice in the distance.

"Grace! Grace! Honey, are you in there?"

It was her dad!

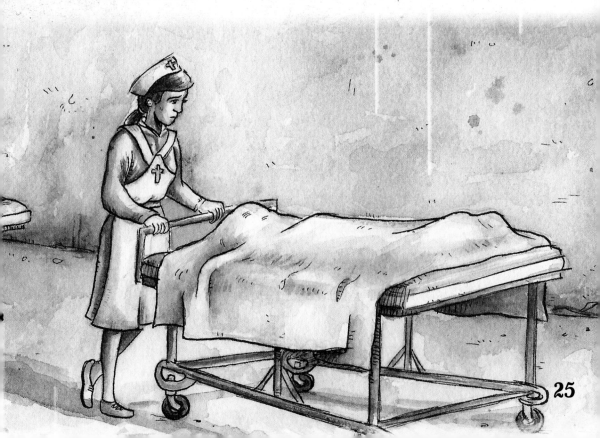

CHAPTER 4

The Good Doctor

"Dad!" screamed Grace. "We're in the tunnel!"

Within seconds, the tunnel was lit up by flashlights. A police officer and Grace's father raced toward her.

"Thank goodness we found you," said Grace's dad. "You've been gone for hours!"

"I'm so sorry, Dad," said Grace. "Bobby got loose and ran into the hospital. I went to look for him, but I got trapped. I hurt my ankle."

Grace began to cry with relief.

"The tunnel was so dark, I was so scared," she sobbed. "But then the doctor found me. He helped me get free, and he fixed up my ankle."

The police officer and Grace's dad lifted her up. Then they carried her from the hospital and sat her on the stone steps outside the building.

"Let's just get you checked over, sweetheart," said the cop. "Then we need to get you to the hospital."

The officer began examining Grace's ankle.

"Who did you say bandaged your ankle, Grace?" she asked. The cop peered at Grace's foot and looked very puzzled.

"The doctor," answered Grace. "The one I met in the tunnel."

"I've never seen splints like this," said the officer. "The ankle is wrapped well, though," she added.

Grace realized she hadn't seen the doctor since her dad and the police officer found her in the tunnel.

"Where is Dr. Akerson?" Grace asked. The police officer looked startled.

"Did you say Dr. Akerson?" she asked.

"Yes," said Grace. "Dr. Walter Akerson. He was so nice." The police officer's face turned white.

"Walter . . . Akerson," the cop said slowly, as if she'd perhaps heard Grace incorrectly. Grace nodded.

"That was my grandfather's name," the officer said. "He worked here at Hilltop Sanatorium for many years. People said he was a very good doctor."

The officer looked very sad.

"When I was a kid, my grandfather told me that many people died here. Back then, they didn't have the medicines they do today. There was nothing the doctors could do to save the patients. My grandfather never forgave himself for not being able to help more people."

The officer and Grace's father lifted Grace up and helped her down the stairs. Then Grace turned back toward the hospital.

"Wait, we have to find Dr. Akerson," she said. "I want to thank him for helping me!"

"But this doesn't make any sense," said the police officer.

"My grandfather died more than 30 years ago."

Just then, Grace saw a small movement in one of the broken windows. In the dim light, she could see a man looking down at her. A man wearing a white coat.

Before Grace could say anything, he melted into the darkness.

Trapped in the Abandoned Hospital

1. Grace is afraid of entering the hospital, but she still does. Why? Use examples from the story to explain.

2. What strange things does Grace see and hear in the hospital that tell her she may not be alone?

3. Why do you think the ghostly voices tell Grace to get out of the tunnel?

4. Before he disappears, Dr. Akerson asks Grace if he's been of help. Why do you think it's important to the doctor that he's helped Grace?

5. What happened in this scene (right)? If Grace had the chance, what do you think she'd say to the doctor?

GLOSSARY

ajar (uh-JAR) partly open

animal shelter (AN-uh-muhl SHEL-tur) a place that houses homeless or lost animals

decaying (dih-KAY-ing) rotting

diagnosis (*dye*-ug-NOH-sis) the identification of a disease or illness

dilapidated (dih-LAP-uh-day-tid) partly ruined from age or lack of care

dismay (diss-MAY) a feeling of alarm or disappointment

gurney (GUR-nee) a flat, padded table with wheels used for transporting patients or bodies

inseparable (in-SEP-ur-uh-buhl) incapable of being separated

sanatorium (san-*uh*-TOHR-ee-uhm) a building where patients suffering from certain long-term diseases stay to increase their health and ease symptoms

shards (SHAHRDZ) broken pieces

splints (SPLINTZ) thin pieces of wood or another sturdy material used to support broken bones

study (STUHD-ee) a room, often with lots of bookshelves, where people read and learn

tuberculosis (too-*bur*-kyuh-LOH-siss) a disease that usually affects the lungs and causes fever, coughing, and difficulty breathing

undertakers (UHN-dur-tay-kurz) people who prepare dead bodies for burial

ward (WARD) an area of a hospital where a certain group of patients is treated

winced (WINSD) shrank back, as from pain

ABOUT THE AUTHOR

Dee Phillips develops and writes nonfiction books for young readers and fiction books—including historical fiction—for middle graders and young adults. She loves to read and write stories that have a twist or an unexpected, thought-provoking ending. Dee lives near the ocean on the southwest coast of England. A keen hiker, her biggest ambition is to one day walk the entire coast of Great Britain.

ABOUT THE ILLUSTRATOR

Anthony Resto graduated from the American Academy of Art with a BFA in Watercolor. He has been illustrating children's books, novellas, and comics for six years, and is currently writing his own children's book. His most recent illustrated books include *Happyland: A Tale in Two Parts* and *Oracle of the Flying Badger*. You can find his other illustrated books and fine art works at Anthonyresto.com. In his free time, he enjoys restoring his vintage RV and preparing for the zombie apocalypse.